Stone Soup

Retold by **Cathy Dubowski**
Illustrated by **Mark Dubowski**

Star Bright Books
New York

Text copyright © 1998 Catherine Dubowski. Illustrations copyright © 1998 Mark Dubowski.
All rights reserved. Published in the United States by Star Bright Books, New York.
ISBN: 887734-22-8 Library of Congress Catalog Card Number 97-23590
Domino Readers and Star Bright Books and their logos are trademarks of Star Bright Books, Inc.
Manufactured in China 0 9 8 7 6 5 4 3 2 1

One day, three men came to a

town. Their names were Will, Bill, and

Dill. They went up to a and

knocked on the door. "We are poor

and hungry," they said. "Can you

please spare some food?"

"No," said the who

opened the door. "We have no

food. We are also poor and hungry."

Will, Bill, and Dill went to the

next . They knocked on the

door. A opened it.

Will, Bill, and Dill said to her,

"Can you please spare some

food? We are poor and hungry."

"No," said the . "Do not

ask for food here. We have no

food to spare, for we are poor and

hungry, too."

Will, Bill, and Dill went to every

in the town. At each

they were told the same thing. "Do

not ask for food here."

Will, Bill, and Dill did not know

what to think. The people did not

look poor. They did not look hungry.

"Well, then," Bill said, "if you

are poor and hungry, we will make

our special  soup for you."

"What?" people cried. "Soup

from a ? We have never

heard of such soup. That will be

something to see!"

   "First we need a big ,"

said Will.

   "I have a big ," a

said. And she quickly ran to get it.

"We need some water, too,"

said Bill.

"I will get the water," said a

. He took the and ran

to fill it with water.

Will, Bill, and Dill made a big . They put the over the .

"Now," said Dill, "we need a good ."

"I will get a ," said a . And he ran to get the .

Will dropped the into the

water in the .

"Now," said Dill, "we need a

big ."

"I will get it," said a .

And he ran to get it. Bill stirred the soup with the . Dill took a little sip of the soup. He stirred the soup with the .

"Well," asked the people, "how is it?"

"*Mmm,*" said Dill, "pretty good. Only . . . it is too bad you do not have any . would make this soup fit for a ."

"I may have some ," said a . And she ran home to get her .

Will put the into the . Bill stirred the soup with the . Dill took a little sip of the soup.

"Well," asked the people, "how is it?"

"*Mmm,*" said Dill, "it is pretty good. Only . . . it is too bad you do not have any .  would make this soup fit for a ."

"I may have some ," said

a . And she ran home to get

her .

Will put the  into the .

Bill stirred the soup in the .

Dill took a little sip of the soup.

"Well," asked the people, "how

is it?"

"*Mmm*," said Dill, "it is pretty

good. Only . . . it is too bad you do

not have any . would

make this soup fit for a ."

"I may have some ," said

a . And he ran home quickly

to get his .

Will put the into the .

Bill stirred the soup with the .

Dill took a little sip of the soup.

"Well," asked the people, "how

is it?"

"*Mmm,*" said Dill, "it is pretty

good." And he took another sip.

"Only . . . it is too bad you do

not have any . would

make this soup fit for a  ."

"I may have some ,"

said a 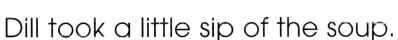. And he ran home

to get his 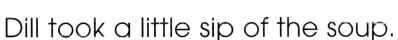.

   Will put the 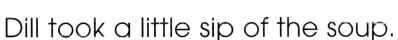 into the 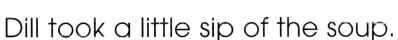.

Bill stirred the soup with the 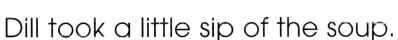.

Dill took a little sip of the soup.

"Well," asked the people, "how is it?"

Dill smiled. Then Bill took a little sip of the soup and he smiled. Then Will took a little sip of the soup and

said with a smile, "This is the best

 soup we have ever made!"

"Hooray!" the people shouted.

And then Will, Bill, and Dill, and all

the people sat down to eat the

 soup.

"Yum!" said a girl. "This soup is so good!"

"Yum!" said a boy. "This soup is truly fit for a ."

"And just think," said a , "we made this good soup from just an old ."

"Will and Bill and Dill are

so smart." Will, Bill, and Dill just

laughed. They ate the good soup

until they were full.

The  soup was good. It was easy to make. And Will, Bill, and Dill knew that as long as they could make soup, they would never go hungry again.